THE USBORNE HISTORY QUIZBOOK

Alastair Smith

Edited by Judy Tatchell

Designed by
Nigel Reece and Richard Johnson

Cover design by Ruth Russell

Illustrated by
Jonathon Heap and Peter Dennis

Additional illustration by
Kuo Kang Chen, Guy Smith and Steve Lings

Consultant: Julie Penn

Contents

About this book

The main part of this book is divided into 12 topics
from history. The topics range from **The dinosaur age**
to **The twentieth century** and each one takes up two
pages. There is lots to read about all these topics,
with quiz questions to answer as you go along.

How to do the quizzes

Within each of the two-page topic sections there are ten quiz questions for you
to answer. These questions are printed in italic type, *like this*. Some of the quiz
questions rely on general knowledge. Others ask you to guess whether a fact is
true or false, or to choose between several possible answers. You will be able to
answer some questions if you study the pictures on the page. Jot your answers on
a piece of paper and check them against the correct answers on pages 28-31.

The Megaquiz

On pages 26-27 is the Megaquiz. This consists
of ten quick quizzes which ask questions about things
you have read about earlier in the book. Again, keep a
note of your answers and then check them against the
Megaquiz answers on page 32.

The dinosaur age

Millions of years ago, strange reptiles called dinosaurs dominated the Earth. They probably appeared about 210 million years ago and died out about 65 million years ago. Humans did not appear until about one million years ago.

Hundreds of different sorts of dinosaurs developed and then died out. Those on this page lived several million years before those opposite.

1. The word dinosaur means:
a) terrible lizard; b) massive teeth;
c) giant feet.

What was Earth like then?

When dinosaurs were alive, most of the land was fairly warm. There were swamps and oases scattered about. Dinosaurs and other reptiles liked these conditions.

2. What do you think this tail was used for?

Were all dinosaurs big?

Not all dinosaurs were big. Some, such as Compsognathus, were no bigger than large turkeys.

Stegosaurus was 7m (23ft) long – but its brain was only as big as a walnut.

Compsognathus

Which was the biggest dinosaur?

The biggest dinosaur was called Brachiosaurus. It ate plants. It was longer than two buses and its footprints would have been big enough for you to sit down in.

5. Brachiosaurus was good at climbing trees. True or false?

Brachiosaurus

6. Nobody knows what colour the dinosaurs were. True or false?

3. Which dinosaur shown on these pages has a name which means Tyrant Lizard King?

Stegosaurus

4. Bones preserved in rock are called:
a) toggles; b) fossils; c) skulls.

How did we get here?

Over millions of years, the Earth's environment changes. Some living things adapt to the changes. This is called evolution. Others do not adapt so they die out.

The Earth is about 4,600 million years old. This panel shows when different living things evolved.

3,000 million years ago.
Bacteria, the first life.

1,500 million years ago.
Algae and jellyfish.

500 million years ago.
Plants

280 million years ago.
Reptiles

200 million years ago.
Dinosaurs and mammals.

Parasaurolophus' head was as long as a man.

Which was the fiercest dinosaur?

Tyrannosaurus rex was the largest meat eater that has ever lived. Its teeth were as long as daggers. It would have been tall enough to look through a first floor window.

8. A meat eater like Tyrannosaurus rex is called: a) a carnivore; b) a herbivore.

9. Was Tyrannosaurus rex the biggest dinosaur?

10. The number of different types of dinosaur found so far is about: a) 6; b) 40; c) 800.

The top of Pachycephalosaurus' head was tougher than a brick. It was useful for butting enemies.

7. How many of the animals shown on these two pages still exist?

Tyrannosaurus rex

The first dinosaur fossil was found over 300 years ago. The finder thought it was a giant's bone.

How is a fossil made?

A dead animal's flesh rots away, leaving only the bony parts.

The bones are buried under mud, sand and rotting plants.

As pressure builds up on top of it, this earthy mixture turns to rock.

Rock

Over millions of years the bones soak up minerals from the rock around them.

The bones become rock (fossilized). Fossils provide clues to what living things looked like long ago.

Why did the dinosaurs die out?

Nobody is certain why dinosaurs died out. A change in climate is the most likely reason. This would have led to a shortage of food.

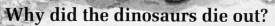

This section shows how humans might have evolved from early sorts of ape.

35 million years ago.
First apes

14 million years ago.
Ramapithecus

5 million years ago.
Man-ape

2 million years ago.
Handy Man

1.5 million years ago.
Upright Man

200 thousand years ago.
Neanderthal Man

40 thousand years ago.
Modern Man

Ancient Egypt

Thousands of years ago, the Ancient Egyptians built huge tombs, called pyramids, for their dead kings and queens. Some pyramids were taller than a 30-storey tower block.

When a king or queen died, the Egyptians preserved the body. They thought this would mean that the dead person's spirit would live forever. They built a pyramid so that the spirit would always have a house on Earth to return to.

By about 1550BC, the Ancient Egyptians had stopped building pyramids. Instead, they buried royalty in tombs cut out of the rock in a valley called the Valley of the Kings.

1. Is there still a country called Egypt?

How was the body preserved?

To preserve the body, some organs were taken out. The skin, bones and other remains were dried, using a salty chemical. This took several weeks. Finally, the body was perfumed and bandaged in cloth. This process is called embalming.

The chief priest, dressed as Anubis, god of the dead, embalmed the body.

2. Embalmed bodies are also known as:
a) dummies;
b) mummies;
c) tummies.

3. The embalmed bodies of some Ancient Egyptians have lasted until today. True or false?

What was the funeral like?

The coffin was put on to a decorated sledge and dragged to the tomb. The sledge looked like a boat. The Egyptians thought the king would need a boat to cross the imaginary water between Earth and heaven.

Boat-like sledge

King's coffin

Adults wore heavy eye make-up. This protected the eye area from the Sun.

How long did it take to build a pyramid?

It took 4,000 workers 20 years to build one of the biggest pyramids. The workers had to spend three months each year working on them.

The Egyptians wanted the pyramids to last forever. Only the best built pyramids are still standing today, though.

The Egyptians could have used more machinery but they built the pyramids mostly by hand. The harder the work, the more honour it did to the ruler. The Egyptians thought their kings were half god, half human.

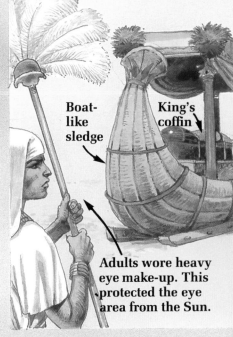

The Egyptians built hundreds of statues like this, called sphinxes. The heads were carved to look like the heads of kings.

Pyramids were covered with white limestone.

Ramps made of rubble and mud spiralled up around the pyramid. Builders dragged the huge stone blocks up these ramps.

5. Where was this stone, called a capstone, going to go?

4. Which of these was not a queen of Egypt: a) Cleopatra; b) Nefertiti; c) Elizabeth I ?

Most adults shaved their hair and wore wigs. This was clean and cool.

Many children had their heads shaved except for a single lock of hair.

Some girls had hair like dreadlocks.

6. What made the pyramids white?

Did you know?

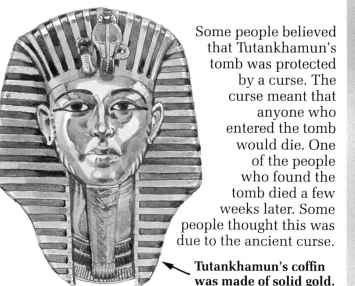

Tutankhamun became king when he was 10 and died when he was 18. His tomb in the Valley of the Kings was discovered in 1922. Most other royal tombs had been robbed over the years but his was untouched.

7. What were Egyptian kings called?

Some people believed that Tutankhamun's tomb was protected by a curse. The curse meant that anyone who entered the tomb would die. One of the people who found the tomb died a few weeks later. Some people thought this was due to the ancient curse.

Tutankhamun's coffin was made of solid gold.

Where were other Egyptians buried?

Most people were buried in the sand on the outskirts of town.

Embalming was so expensive that only rich people could afford it.

8. What did Egyptian children usually wear in the summer?

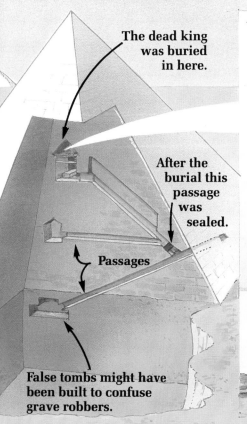

The dead king was buried in here.

After the burial this passage was sealed.

Passages

False tombs might have been built to confuse grave robbers.

What was on the tomb walls?

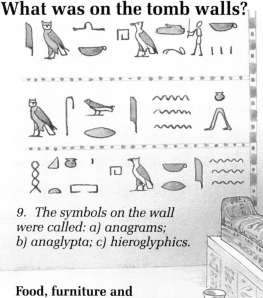

9. The symbols on the wall were called: a) anagrams; b) anaglypta; c) hieroglyphics.

Food, furniture and embalmed bodies of the king's pets.

10. Which of the symbols on the wall means "to walk"?

On the tomb walls were carved rows of pictures and symbols. This was a sort of writing. It told stories of the king's life and explained to his spirit how it should find its way to heaven.

Most of what we know about the Ancient Egyptians was discovered from picture-writing in pyramids and rock-cut tombs.

The coffin had a sculpture of the dead king's face on it.

Ancient Greece

About 2,500 years ago, Greece was made up of many cities. Each one ruled the countryside around it. What it was like to be alive then depended a lot on where you lived.

A wealthy person in the city of Athens, for instance, would have a comfortable life, with visits to the theatre and parties to go to. A young man in Sparta would be a soldier living in a grim barracks.

1. What is the capital of Greece now, Athens or Sparta?

What were Greek plays like?

You could watch two sorts of play in a Greek theatre. They were called tragedies and comedies. Women were not allowed to act so men had to dress up to play female roles.

Tragedies were about the fates of past Greek heroes and were serious. Actors wore masks to show the age, sex and mood of a character.

Comedies often made fun of politicians and important people.

2. What moods do these masks show?

Some Ancient Greek plays have been translated into English and are still performed.

Who was in charge of Athens?

Athens is famous for its system of government, called democracy. Each citizen could vote on how the city was run. Unfortunately, the Greeks did not allow women or slaves to be citizens, so they did not have a vote.

Today, countries are called democracies if everyone can vote to choose political leaders.

Architects ever since have copied the elegant style of Ancient Greek buildings. The style is known as "classical".

A political meeting.

3. It was a crime to chop down an olive tree in Athens. True or false?

The ruin of this theatre is still standing in Athens. It held 14,000 people.

The stage was here.

Who was Homer?

Homer was a Greek poet who might have lived about 800BC. He made up long poems about mythical Greek heroes. Two of his poems, the *Iliad* and the *Odyssey*, have survived until now. The *Iliad* is about the legendary Trojan War.

4. Homer's poems were called:
a) epics; b) topics; c) episodes.

What was the Trojan War about?

A Trojan prince called Paris kidnapped Helen, the beautiful wife of Menelaus. Menelaus and his brother Agamemnon, a Greek king, raised an army and sailed to the city of Troy to fetch her back. There were 1,000 ships in the fleet which carried the army.

The Greeks besieged Troy for ten years without success. Then Odysseus, a Greek general, had a plan. The Greeks built a huge model horse and led the Trojans to believe it was a gift to the gods. They left the horse outside Troy and pretended to sail away.

Who were the Greek gods?

The Greek gods behaved a bit like humans – they got jealous, argued and played tricks. However, they had magic powers so they could change shape, make things happen and get from one place to another in a flash.

7. Guess which god is which:
a) Poseidon, god of the sea;
b) Aphrodite, goddess of love;

c) Zeus, king of the gods;
d) Athene, goddess of wisdom.

How were children treated in Sparta?

Spartan boys were brought up to be the toughest soldiers in Greece. Girls also trained to be strong so that they would have good warrior sons. The Spartans wanted to be able to resist any invasion or slave rebellion.

Boys were sent away to an army training school at the age of seven. They were taught to read and write but learning to use weapons was more important. They also had dancing lessons to make them strong and agile.

There is a story that the boys were underfed and had to steal extra food from local farms. If they were caught they were beaten by teachers – not for stealing, but for getting caught.

8. Before battle, Spartan soldiers put perfume in their hair. True or false?

Why were the Greeks keen on sport?

The Greeks were often at war. Fit, strong men made better soldiers so they exercised regularly at sports centres, called *gymnasia*.

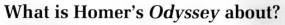

Athletics festivals were held in stadiums like this.

Athletics festivals were held in honour of the gods. The most famous one was held every four years in the city of Olympia. People came from all over Greece to compete.

9. Can you identify these four sports, all played by the Ancient Greeks?

Did you know?

If the sports festival at Olympia started during a war, fighting was stopped so that soldiers could go and take part.

10. Which modern sports festival is named after the Games at Olympia?

The winners were given these prizes:

Palm branches   **Olive wreath**

Ribbons

The Trojans took the horse into the city to please the gods. However, Greek soldiers were hiding inside. That night, they climbed out, and opened the city gates. The Greeks raided the city and won the war.

5. What was the horse made of?

What is Homer's *Odyssey* about?

The *Odyssey* is about Odysseus' adventures on his way home after the Trojan War.

He had to outwit the Sirens who lured sailors to their deaths on the rocks by singing beautifully.

Sirens had the faces of beautiful women, with birds' bodies and clawed feet.

He had to escape from Circe, a witch who turned men into animals, and kill a terrifying one-eyed monster.

6. Odysseus took: a) one week; b) two days; c) ten years to get home.

Ancient Rome

Two thousand years ago, Rome was the most important city in Europe. It was the centre of a huge empire which ruled over much of Europe and the Mediterranean lands.

What were Roman baths?

Roman baths were not like modern swimming baths. They had several pools, all at different temperatures. Bathers went from one to another. This left them feeling very clean and refreshed. Men and women went to the baths at different times of day.

1. Unscramble the name of this famous Roman ruler: luiJus Carsae.

A slave working as a hair plucker. It was fashionable to have a smooth, hairless body.

A slave giving a massage.

2. Rome is now the capital of which European country?

Did you know?

To get clean the Romans covered themselves in olive oil, which they then scraped off with a scraper, called a *strigilis*. It worked just as well as soap.

Warm bath

This furnace heated a tank of water. The water was pumped to the hot bath, warm bath and steam room. The furnace was tended by a slave.

Hot bath

What did Romans do for entertainment?

In Rome, fights were put on for the public to watch. These fights were called the Games. The loser was often killed in the fight. If not, the crowd voted whether or not he should be put to death. A brave loser might be allowed to live.

3. Which month is named after Mars, the Roman god of war?

The crowd gave this sign if they wanted the loser to live.

Who took part in the fights?

The fighters were criminals or prisoners of war. They might be forced to fight against wild animals, professional fighters or each other.

4. What sign did people give if they wanted the loser to die?

5. Professional fighters were called: a) gladiators; b) exterminators; c) mashpotaters.

The biggest Games arena in Rome was the Colosseum. It held 48,000 people. This is what it looks like now.

Where were chariot races held?

Chariot races were held in a massive stadium called the Circus Maximus. It held about 280,000 people. Chariot racers belonged to different teams. Supporters in the crowd wore the colours of their favourite team. There were even supporters' clubs to join.

6. The Circus Maximus was larger than any soccer stadium. True or false?

Most crashes happened on the sharp bends.

In the steam room people sweated a lot. This was like a sauna.

Chariots were very light so that they would go fast.

The horses' reins were tied around the driver. If the chariot crashed, the driver had to cut himself free with a hooked knife.

Changing room

9. The Romans spoke: a) Latin; b) Greek; c) Turkish.

Food seller with sausages and honey cakes.

Where did slaves come from?

Most slaves were prisoners of war that the Roman army captured on their foreign campaigns. They were brought back to Rome to do the worst jobs in return for their keep.

7. Can you see three different jobs that slaves are doing at the baths?

The cold bath (frigidarium) was for cooling off after the hot baths or exercise.

8. What is this building?

10. Roman men wore trousers. True or false?

The Vikings

The Vikings came from the far north of Europe. About 1,200 years ago they began exploring the world in search of riches.

Some Vikings raided towns and villages and stole what they wanted. Others traded peacefully in foreign towns.

1. Can you name any of the countries where the Vikings came from?

2. What weapon did the Vikings use most often?

What was a Viking raid like?

Vikings tried to catch their victims by surprise. They did not want to waste their energy on a hard fight.

3. How many Vikings have been killed on this raid?

They took prisoners and killed anyone who got in the way. Important prisoners were held to ransom. Poor prisoners were taken back home to be slaves.

Viking ships, called longships, were flat-bottomed so that they could be sailed into shallow waters. This made surprise attacks easier.

4. What were the holes in the roofs of houses for?

Where did Vikings trade?

The Vikings traded mainly with places which they could reach by ship. They founded trading towns all over Europe, such as Dublin in Ireland and Kiev in the Ukraine. Many Vikings settled in trading towns.

7. The name Viking comes from a Viking word meaning: a) King Vic; b) adventurer; c) red beard.

How far did they travel?

Vikings were such good sailors that they even reached North America. They travelled about 7,000 miles there and back. It was 400 years before any other Europeans went there.

8. Which was further away from the Vikings' home, Ireland or North America?

Some traders did not like the Vikings – they thought that the Vikings swore, fought and got drunk too often.

Vikings loved Arabian silks and cloths like these.

Treasures from a raid.

The Vikings usually went on raids in the summer, when the weather was good for sailing. They liked to attack monasteries and churches because these had silver and gold treasures.

5. *How did the Vikings make their ships move?*

How did the Vikings celebrate?

When they got home, the Vikings held huge feasts that went on for days. Poets called bards told long, exciting stories about famous battles and adventures.

6. *The stories were called: a) sagas; b) lagers; c) lyrics.*

Bard

Did you know?

Vikings often took their sons with them on trading voyages. That way the boys learned how to be skilful sailors.

Slaves

How were Vikings buried?

Important warriors were buried or burned in their ships. The Vikings believed that the person's soul sailed to Viking heaven in the ship. There, men fought all day. Every evening there was a huge feast.

9. *Viking heaven was called: a) Valhalla; b) Hell; c) Iceland.*

Vikings thought that to die of natural causes was boring and cowardly. They called it a "straw death". The best way to die was in battle.

10. *Which weekday is named after Thor, the Viking god of thunder?*

11

The Crusades

The Crusades were wars between groups of Christians and Moslems. They began in 1096 and lasted on and off for the next 200 years. The wars were about who should rule Syria and Palestine (see map on the right).

Why was this area important?

Jerusalem in Palestine was a holy place for Moslems. They believed that their leader, Mohammed, rose to heaven from Jerusalem.

1. Why was there a wall around Jerusalem?

Palestine was important to Christians because Jesus Christ had lived there. Christians called the area the Holy Land. They made journeys, called pilgrimages, to pray there.

2. Where was Jesus Christ born?

A map showing ITALY, GREECE, SYRIA, PALESTINE, Jerusalem, Bethlehem, Mediterranean Sea, EGYPT, with insets of a Moslem soldier and a Christian soldier.

Why did the Crusades begin?

Before the Crusades, Moslems had ruled Palestine for centuries. The Moslems had let Christian pilgrims visit the area safely.

In 1076, though, another Moslem group called the Seljuk Turks took over Palestine. They killed Christians they found there.

In 1096, the Pope, who was head of the Christian Church, asked Christians to take the Holy Land from the Seljuks. He said that if they did, God would forgive all their sins.

About 50,000 people set off from all over Europe. Whole families joined the Crusade, most of them poor. They thought that Palestine was a rich land where they would make a good living. This Crusade was called the People's Crusade.

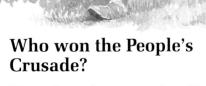

The army travelled over 2,000 miles to the Holy Land, mostly on foot.

Who won the People's Crusade?

Many Crusaders starved or died of disease on the way. The Seljuks killed those who got there.

3. 20,000 people died on the way to the Holy Land. True or false?

Did the Christians ever win?

Three years after the start of the People's Crusade, another army of Crusaders captured the Holy Land. It was difficult for them to keep order, though, because most of the people there were Moslems. Bit by bit, the Moslems won the area back.

4. The Moslems had faster horses than the Crusaders. True or false?

Who led the armies?

The Moslem general who won back most of the Holy Land from the Christians was called Saladin. He was a brilliant general and he was fierce but he treated his enemies fairly.

Richard the Lionheart (King Richard I of England) led a Crusade against Saladin. Although he lost the war, Saladin promised to allow pilgrims to visit Jerusalem. Saladin and Richard respected each other although they were enemies.

5. Saladin's sword was called: a) a scimitar; b) a scythe; c) a scarab.

6. Why was Richard I nicknamed "the Lionheart"?

How did the Crusades change Europe?

Crusaders brought back types of food and other goods that were new to Europe. Some of these are shown in the picture.

7. Which of these did the Crusaders NOT bring back to Europe: a) oranges; b) potatoes; c) pepper?

Moslem castles were very strong so European castle-builders copied them. (See next page.)

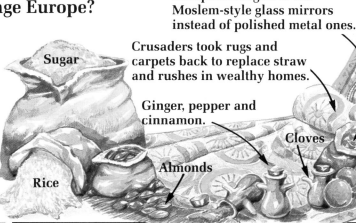

Europeans began to use Moslem-style glass mirrors instead of polished metal ones.

Crusaders took rugs and carpets back to replace straw and rushes in wealthy homes.

Ginger, pepper and cinnamon.

Sugar

Rice

Almonds

Cloves

Silk

Dates

Figs

Raisins

English castle before the Crusades.

Moslem castle

Did you know?

The way numbers are written developed from symbols used by Moslem mathematicians.

8. The numbers on the right were used by Moslem mathematicians. Can you match them to the modern numbers above them?

9   7   4   1

١٣٤٧٩

How big was the Moslem Empire?

This map shows how big the Moslem Empire was during the Crusades.

9. The Moslems ruled parts of three continents. True or false?

Moslems occupied parts of Spain from the 7th to the 15th century. You can still see Moslem buildings in Spain, such as the

Palace of Alhambra in Granada. This was started in 1230.

10. The game below was first played in Europe by Moslems. What is it?

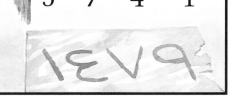

Syria and Palestine

Spain

Moslem Empire (in red).

Palace of Alhambra

A medieval castle

Medieval castles in Europe were the homes of rulers and wealthy landowners. They protected the owner, his subjects and possessions from local bandits or invading armies.

During the 13th century, Crusaders brought back ideas from the Middle East for how to improve medieval European castles. Features marked with a star (★) show some of these ideas.

Where were castles built?

Most castles were built on steep hills or cliffs. This made them difficult to attack. It also gave the defenders a good view of the surrounding countryside so that they could see approaching enemies.

1. Where did the castle defenders get water to drink from?

Did castles take long to build?

It could take 3,000 builders ten years to build a big castle.

The walls could be up to 5m (16ft) thick.

Turrets made good look-out points.

Well

★ The inner wall is higher than the outer wall. This is so that guards on the inner wall can fire down over the outer wall at enemies close by.

If attackers break into the castle, they can be trapped in this passage. Defenders shut the gates and then shoot them through the holes above.

2. This strong gatehouse is called: a) a barbecue; b) a pelican; c) a barbican.

Food stocks

3. These holes are called: a) murder holes; b) peep holes; c) man holes.

Castle archers shoot out through these narrow slits, called loops. It is difficult for enemies to shoot back through them.

Notches, called crenels, in the battlements let soldiers lean out to shoot at the enemy.

Shutters give extra protection.

Defenders duck behind merlons to avoid return fire.

★ The picture of the wall is cut away to show a permanent stone overhang with holes in the floor. It is called a machicolation. Soldiers shoot or drop rocks through the holes.

★ These overhanging wooden shelters are called hourds. They are put up for defence and used like machicolations (see below left).

What was a siege?

During a siege, attackers surrounded a castle to stop anyone from entering or leaving it. The people inside could survive for months if they had fresh water and plenty of food stored up.

Attackers hoped that a long siege would cause the people inside to run out of food or get ill. They might just get tired of fighting.

4. The longest siege lasted for six months. True or false?

Did you know?

Once cannons had been invented, castles were no longer so safe. Cannonballs could blast huge holes in the walls. Cannons were invented in the 14th century.

5. The explosive that fired a cannon was: a) dynamite; b) gunpowder.

6. Gunpowder was invented by the Chinese. True or false?

What weapons did attackers use?

Attackers used huge catapults, called mangonels and trebuchets. These hurled heavy objects into the castle or at its walls. Sometimes dead and rotting animals were flung into the castle to spread disease.

7. Put these weapons in order of invention: a) mangonel; b) tank; c) spear.

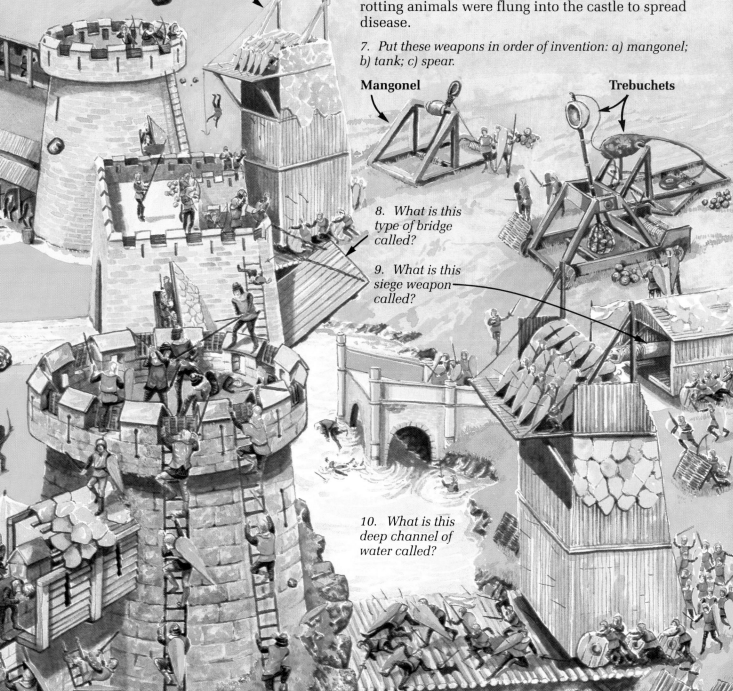

Scaling tower

Mangonel

Trebuchets

8. What is this type of bridge called?

9. What is this siege weapon called?

10. What is this deep channel of water called?

The Aztecs and the Incas

About 500 years ago much of Central and South America was ruled by two powerful tribes, the Aztecs and the Incas. They worshipped the Sun and had so much gold that they even used it to decorate gardens. Less than 50 years later, though, their empires had disappeared. They had been destroyed by Spanish conquerors who came in search of fabulous wealth.

Aztec Empire

Tenochtitlan

Cuzco

Inca Empire

Who were the Aztecs?

The Aztecs ruled several other tribes in part of what is now Mexico. Their king was called the Great Speaker. He had a deputy called Snake Woman. These two people stood for the man and woman who had created the Earth.

Did you know?

The post of Snake Woman was always held by a man. This was because only men were allowed to rule in the Aztec kingdom.

1. The South Americans sometimes ate guinea pigs. True or false?

What did Aztecs wear?

The more important someone was, the grander the clothes they were allowed to wear. It was illegal for a lowly person to copy a powerful person's clothing.

What was the Aztec capital city?

The Aztec capital was called Tenochtitlan. It was built on an island in the middle of a lake. It had a main square with temples and palaces round it.

2. The capital of present-day Mexico is called: a) Tenochtitlan; b) Mexico City; c) Los Angeles.

The Great Temple

Warrior

3. Which of these people did the Aztecs think was the most important: a) warrior; b) farmer; c) weaver?

Where was the Inca kingdom?

The Inca kingdom ran down the west of South America. It was larger than the Aztec Empire. The Inca king, Sapa Inca, lived in Cuzco, the capital city. Most people in the Inca kingdom were farmers or craftspeople.

How did the Incas travel?

Incas travelled on foot. A huge network of tracks criss-crossed the Empire. There were huts, called rest houses, a day's walk apart so that travellers had somewhere to spend the night.

Rest house

Bridge made from thick rope.

Steps were built up steep hills.

Runners carried messages from town to town.

There were no horses in America. Incas used these animals to carry heavy loads, instead.

9. What is this animal?

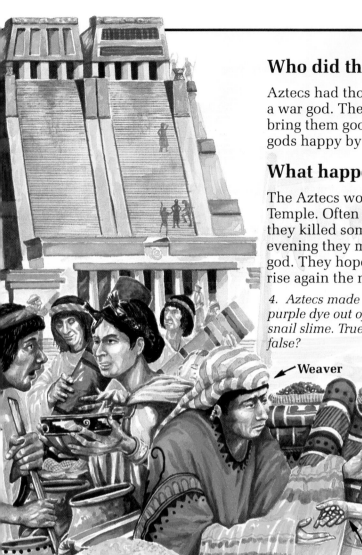

Who did the Aztecs worship?

Aztecs had thousands of gods, from a flower god to a war god. The Aztecs believed that the gods could bring them good or bad luck. They tried to keep the gods happy by giving them gifts.

What happened in the Great Temple?

The Aztecs worshipped their gods in the Great Temple. Often they made a human sacrifice, that is, they killed someone as an offering to a god. Every evening they made a human sacrifice to the Sun god. They hoped this would mean the Sun would rise again the next morning.

4. Aztecs made purple dye out of sea snail slime. True or false?

6. Which Aztec god is this?

← **Weaver**

Farmer ↗

Cocoa beans

5. Which is worth more, the bird or the rug?

What happened in the market?

In the market in the main square, Aztecs swapped one sort of goods for another. They used cocoa beans as small change if one half of the swap was worth more than the other.

7. Swapping goods instead of selling them is called: a) bartering; b) bantering; c) battering.

8. This bird is: a) a toucan; b) an albatross; c) a turkey.

Why did the empires collapse?

Spanish invaders, called *conquistadores*, first reached Central and South America early in the 16th century. They had several advantages over the Aztecs and Incas, as shown below.

Aztecs and Incas had not seen horses before.

Aztecs and Incas always travelled on foot. The Spaniards had horses, so they could travel much faster along the Inca tracks.

Aztec and Inca warriors.

Spanish weapons.

The Spaniards had guns. Aztecs and Incas only had arrows, knives, spears and clubs.

Aztec and Inca weapons.

The Aztecs and Incas had no resistance to European diseases which the Spaniards brought with them. As a result, thousands died of illnesses such as colds, flu and measles.

Who took over South America?

The *conquistadores* were the first Europeans to explore South America. Some set up their own kingdoms. Many boundaries of present-day South American countries can be traced back to these Spanish kingdoms.

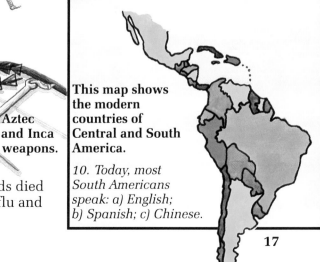

This map shows the modern countries of Central and South America.

10. Today, most South Americans speak: a) English; b) Spanish; c) Chinese.

Inventions and discoveries

People don't always welcome new inventions and discoveries. Here are some important or useful ones which were unpopular at first.

When did people disagree about trousers?

An American called Amelia Bloomer designed trousers for women in 1853.

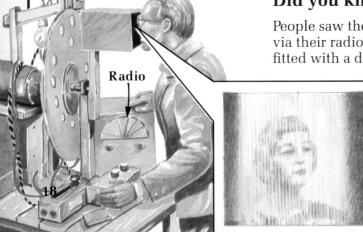

In those days, smartly dressed women had to wear bulky dresses. Many people thought that trousers should only be worn by men. It was a hundred years before trousers for women became fashionable.

1. What were the trousers designed by Amelia Bloomer called?

2. What type of hat is the man wearing?

This is what Amelia Bloomer's trousers looked like.

Who was imprisoned for a discovery?

In the 1630s, Galileo, an Italian scientist, wrote a book supporting the discovery that the Earth and the other planets travel around the Sun.

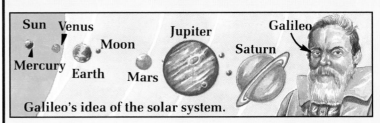

Sun Venus Mercury Earth Moon Mars Jupiter Saturn Galileo

Galileo's idea of the solar system.

This made the leaders of the Catholic Church angry. They believed that the Earth was the centre of the Universe and that the Sun and the other planets went round the Earth.

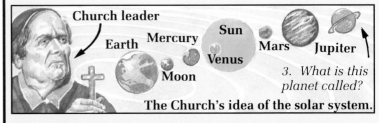

Church leader Earth Mercury Venus Moon Sun Mars Jupiter

3. What is this planet called?

The Church's idea of the solar system.

Galileo was accused of lying and put on trial. He was forced to plead guilty and was imprisoned in his own home.

4. Was Galileo right or wrong?

Why did steam engines cause riots?

Machinery powered by steam engines was first used on farms and in factories in the early 19th century. Each machine did the job of several workers, so many lost their jobs. There were riots as a result. Usually the workers tried to destroy the steam engine during the riot, as shown here.

5. Can you think of another way steam engines were used, apart from on farms and in factories?

Did you know?

Radio

People saw the first TV broadcast via their radios. The radios were fitted with a device to pick up the TV signals. Only a few people saw the first pictures. They showed a person sitting down.

TV pictures are made up of rows of dots. Modern TVs have over 600 rows.

6. The first regular TV broadcasts were made in: a) 1336; b) 1936; c) 1986.

What is this cartoon about?

The cartoon above made fun of a doctor called Edward Jenner, in 1802. He had found a way to prevent people catching a deadly disease called smallpox. He injected patients with germs from a similar but non-deadly disease called cowpox. People who had been injected did not catch smallpox.

People found this discovery, called inoculation, hard to believe. Nowadays, though, inoculation is used to prevent hundreds of different illnesses.

7. Dairymaids often caught cowpox. True or false?

8. Which of these illnesses cannot be prevented by inoculation: a) flu; b) measles; c) a cold?

Why was Charles Darwin unpopular?

About 130 years ago the scientist Charles Darwin made himself unpopular because he disagreed with a story from the Bible. The story told how God created the Earth and everything on it in six days.

Darwin said that over thousands of years the Earth's environment changes. Animals and plants have to adapt in order to survive. Some die out but those that adapt become more efficient. Darwin gave many examples of this process, called evolution (see pages 2-3).

Powerful beak to crush seeds and nuts.

Sharp, strong beak to dig into cacti and chew seeds.

Thin beak to probe for insects and pierce fruit.

One of Darwin's examples came from a study of birds on an island in the Pacific Ocean. He found that similar birds had developed different beaks to eat various types of food.

9. These birds are all types of: a) finch; b) parrot; c) ostrich.

Why was nuclear power unpopular?

Nuclear fuel was first used in power stations in the 1950s. If the fuel leaks, it poisons everything that it touches, even the air. Many people were worried about this and went on demonstrations to protest against nuclear power.

Until the 1950s, most power stations ran on oil or coal. These are safer to use than nuclear fuel but the supply may run out eventually. Also, the smoke from them dissolves in the rain. When the rain falls it damages pastures and forests. This sort of rain is called acid rain.

In 1986, nuclear fuel leaked from a power station at Chernobyl in the Ukraine. The environment for several miles around was ruined. It is still not safe for people to live near Chernobyl, eat food grown there or drink water from the region.

10. Put these inventions in order: a) nuclear power; b) steam power; c) electricity.

The red area shows how far the wind blew the nuclear pollution. Scientists had to check that the areas were safe for people and animals.

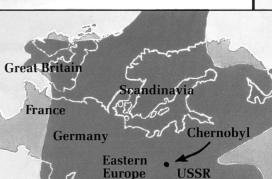

Great Britain

Scandinavia

France

Germany

Chernobyl

Eastern Europe

USSR

Italy

The Wild West

There used to be hundreds of American Indian tribes in North America. As European settlers arrived, they began to take over Indian land. By the 19th century, much of the land was being used for huge cattle ranches, worked on by cowboys.

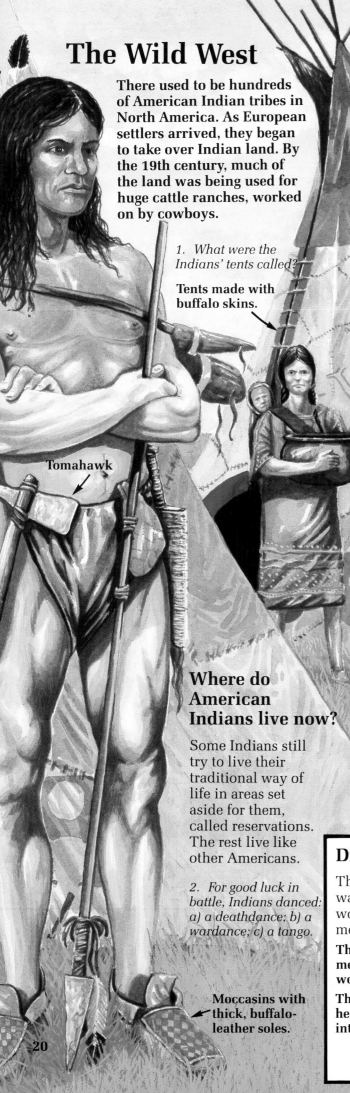

1. What were the Indians' tents called?

Tents made with buffalo skins.

Tomahawk

Where do American Indians live now?

Some Indians still try to live their traditional way of life in areas set aside for them, called reservations. The rest live like other Americans.

2. For good luck in battle, Indians danced: a) a deathdance; b) a wardance; c) a tango.

Moccasins with thick, buffalo-leather soles.

How did the Indians live?

Many tribes trailed herds of buffalo all over the prairies. When hunting, Indians often wore the skins of other animals. This disguised them and their scent from the prey.

What did cowboys do?

Cowboys worked on huge cattle farms, called ranches. The biggest cattle herds had over 15,000 cattle. Cowboys used horses to get around the ranches to check the cattle. The horse usually belonged to the ranch owner but the cowboy owned his own saddle. Cowboys spent most of their working life in the saddle.

3. These cattle are: a) blackhorn cattle; b) shorthorn cattle; c) longhorn cattle.

Why did Indians and cowboys fight?

Ranch owners took over land where Indians had lived for centuries. Sometimes, cowboys used force to push the Indians and the buffalo which they hunted off the ranches. The Indians might attack the ranches in revenge.

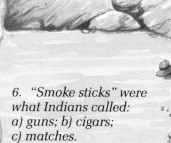

6. "Smoke sticks" were what Indians called: a) guns; b) cigars; c) matches.

Did you know?

The feathers and warpaint that Indians wore had special meanings.

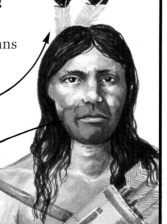

This head-dress meant he had been wounded in battle.

This paint meant he would chase intruders away.

India

20

Buffalo

Arrow heads were barbed so that they would stick into the victim and not fall out.

The best Indian hunters could crawl right up to an animal without it noticing.

Who were the cowboys?

Most cowboys were young, unmarried men. They usually slept in dormitories at the ranch. Ten good cowboys could manage a herd of 1,000 cattle.

The wide hat brim kept the sun out of the cowboy's eyes.

8. Most cowboys wore hats called: a) stetsons; b) top hats; c) bowlers.

Bandana

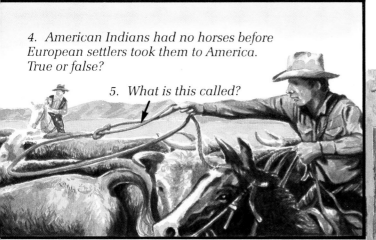

4. American Indians had no horses before European settlers took them to America. True or false?

5. What is this called?

Winchester rifle

Six-shooter

9. Why was the pistol called a six-shooter?

Leather leggings, called chaps, protected trousers and legs from brush and barbed wire.

Why were they called "Red Indians"?

North America

Spain

South America

American Indians used to be called Red Indians. The explorer Christopher Columbus gave them this name. 500 years ago he sailed from Spain to find a sea route to India. Instead, he landed in America. He thought he had reached India, and that the people he met were Indians, although their skin was a slightly redder shade of brown.

7. Which two of these countries now make up North America: USA, Peru, Canada, Brazil, Chile?

Brand for marking cattle.

Spur

10. Why were cattle branded?

21

Trains, cars and planes

Before the invention of trains, cars and planes, a journey that now takes hours could take days or even weeks.

People travelled overland either on foot, on horseback or in horsedrawn carriages. Roads were dirt tracks. When they were dry they were hard and bumpy. When they were wet they became deep, sticky bogs.

1. How many different forms of transport can you see on these two pages?

When did the first passenger train run?

The first passenger train service was in Kent in southern England. It opened in 1830 with a journey only 1.6km (1 mile) long. A steam engine, called Invicta, pulled the train at about 20kmph (12mph).

Some scientists warned that people's bodies might fall apart due to the vibrations of the train.

Most carriages had no roofs.

Invicta

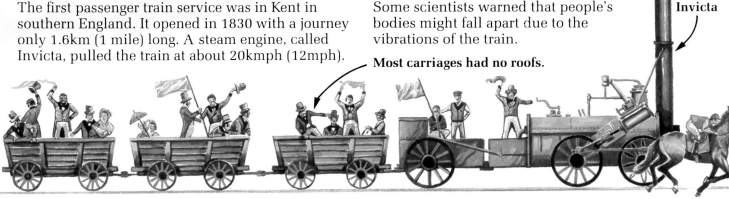

2. The first trains were slower than a galloping horse. True or false?

Did you know?

The longest railway line is over 9,000km (5,600 miles) long. It was built between 1891 and 1905 and stretched from the west to the east of the Russian Empire.

By 1916 there were over 400,000km (250,000 miles) of railway in the USA.

3. The Russian Empire is now known as: a) the USSR; b) the USA; c) the UK.

RUSSIAN EMPIRE

Moscow

Nakhodka

CHINA

What was the first car like?

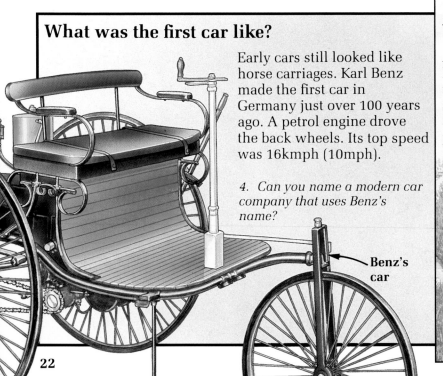

Early cars still looked like horse carriages. Karl Benz made the first car in Germany just over 100 years ago. A petrol engine drove the back wheels. Its top speed was 16kmph (10mph).

4. Can you name a modern car company that uses Benz's name?

Benz's car

Were cars popular?

At first most people hated cars. They said they were dirty, noisy and a danger to horses and people. For many years after the car's invention only rich people could afford them.

Early car

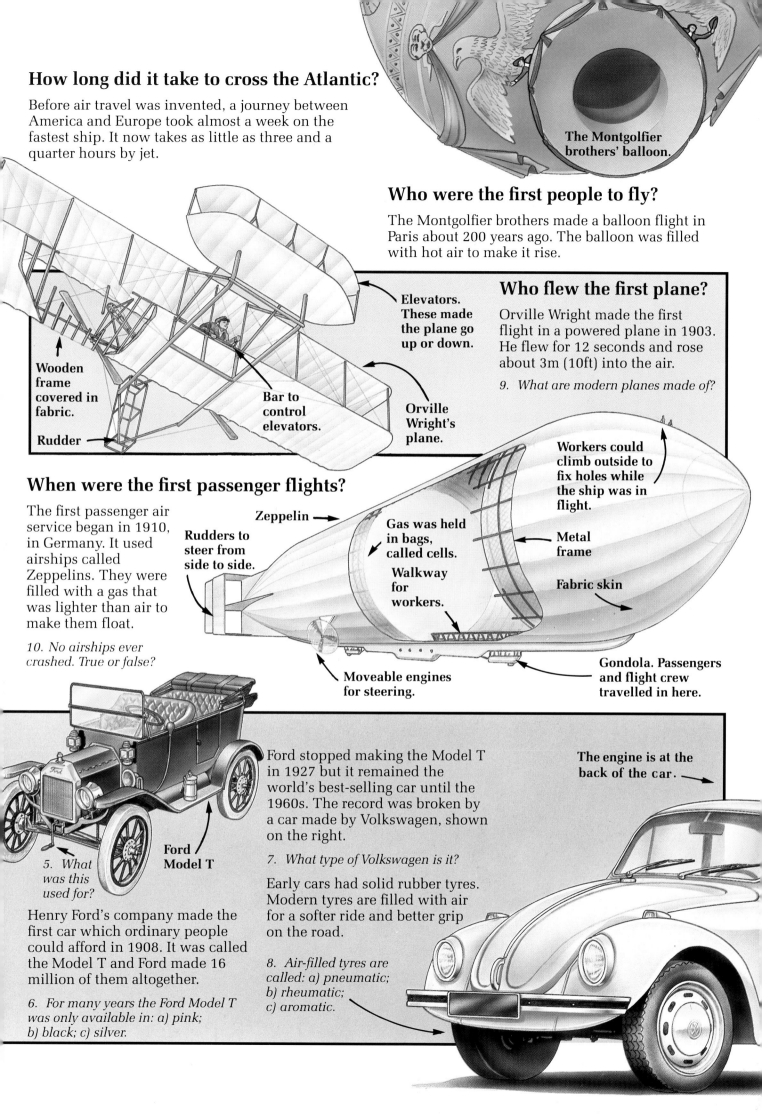

How long did it take to cross the Atlantic?

Before air travel was invented, a journey between America and Europe took almost a week on the fastest ship. It now takes as little as three and a quarter hours by jet.

The Montgolfier brothers' balloon.

Who were the first people to fly?

The Montgolfier brothers made a balloon flight in Paris about 200 years ago. The balloon was filled with hot air to make it rise.

Elevators. These made the plane go up or down.

Who flew the first plane?

Orville Wright made the first flight in a powered plane in 1903. He flew for 12 seconds and rose about 3m (10ft) into the air.

9. What are modern planes made of?

Wooden frame covered in fabric.

Rudder

Bar to control elevators.

Orville Wright's plane.

Workers could climb outside to fix holes while the ship was in flight.

Metal frame

Fabric skin

When were the first passenger flights?

The first passenger air service began in 1910, in Germany. It used airships called Zeppelins. They were filled with a gas that was lighter than air to make them float.

10. No airships ever crashed. True or false?

Zeppelin →

Rudders to steer from side to side.

Gas was held in bags, called cells.

Walkway for workers.

Moveable engines for steering.

Gondola. Passengers and flight crew travelled in here.

Ford stopped making the Model T in 1927 but it remained the world's best-selling car until the 1960s. The record was broken by a car made by Volkswagen, shown on the right.

The engine is at the back of the car. →

7. What type of Volkswagen is it?

Early cars had solid rubber tyres. Modern tyres are filled with air for a softer ride and better grip on the road.

8. Air-filled tyres are called: a) pneumatic; b) rheumatic; c) aromatic.

Ford Model T

5. What was this used for?

Henry Ford's company made the first car which ordinary people could afford in 1908. It was called the Model T and Ford made 16 million of them altogether.

6. For many years the Ford Model T was only available in: a) pink; b) black; c) silver.

The twentieth century

There have probably been more changes since 1900 than during any other century. On these pages, you can read about some of the events which have taken place this century.

What was the Russian Revolution about?

Lenin, the Bolshevik leader, speaking to factory workers.

A factory run by the new government.

Tsar Nicholas II with his family.

Before the Revolution, the emperor of Russia, called the tsar, chose the government from among his noblemen and favourites. The leaders of the Revolution, called the Bolsheviks, wanted a government made up of ordinary people. They thought this would be better for most Russians.

The Bolsheviks seized power in 1917. The new government owned and ran every business in the country. They thought that this would benefit everyone. The system was called communism.

1. What colour was the Bolshevik flag?

In 1918, Tsar Nicholas II was shot by Bolshevik supporters. In 1923, the Russian Empire became known as the Union of Soviet Socialist Republics, or USSR. It was the first communist country.

2. The USSR has not had a tsar since 1918. True or false?

Who were the Nazis?

The Nazis were a German political party. They governed Germany from 1933 to 1945. They promised to make Germany powerful again after years of hardship following World War I.

The man in the photograph (left) was the leader of the Nazi party.

3. What was his name?

How did World War II begin?

During the late 1930s, the Nazis began to take over parts of Europe. In 1939, Britain and France declared war on Germany to try to stop them. Germany continued to invade other countries.

Denmark Norway
Holland
Belgium
France
Germany

Countries invaded by Germany before World War II.

Countries invaded by Germany in the first year of World War II.

Poland: invaded in 1939.

Czechoslovakia: invaded in 1938.

Austria: taken over in 1938.

The German army invaded Holland in 1940.

In 1941, the USA and USSR joined Britain and France. In 1945, Germany surrendered.

4. How long did World War II last?

Did you know?

The first nuclear weapon was used during World War II. It was a bomb dropped by the USA on Hiroshima in Japan in 1945. Japan was on Germany's side in World War II.

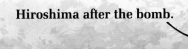
Hiroshima after the bomb.

5. There have been: a) two; b) five; c) 23 World Wars.

What was the Cultural Revolution?

Communists took power in China in 1949, after fighting the old government for over 20 years. By the mid-1960s, they felt that people were forgetting the true aims of communism. They started a scheme which was supposed to increase support for Chinese communism. It was called the Cultural Revolution.

The government banned plays and books which were in favour of life before communism. New books and plays had to praise Chinese communism or say that life had been unfair before it.

6. A war between people of the same country is called: a) a star war; b) a civil war; c) a cold war.

Leaders of the Cultural Revolution sent gangs of young people around China to smash up reminders of the old way of life. The gangs, called the Red Guards, also attacked people who opposed communism.

7. Which was the first country to have a communist government?

An inspector sacks a teacher who criticized communism.

In schools, teachers had to praise Chinese communism to their pupils.

This is a play in favour of communism being performed during the Cultural Revolution.

Red Guards burning books about life before communism.

The Red Guards killed thousands of people. They were finally banned in 1969.

When were computers invented?

The first computer was built during World War II. It was designed to crack secret codes used by the German and Japanese armies.

During the 1950s and 1960s, scientists invented smaller and smaller components until thousands could be fitted into a space the size of a fingernail.

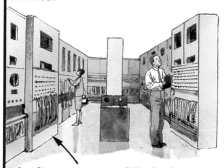

The first computer filled a large room because its electronic parts, called components, were so big.

Components are held inside here on a slice of glass-like material called silicon.

8. This is called: a) a bug; b) a byte; c) a chip.

Computers have become smaller and cheaper but also more powerful than early ones.

Who made the first space flight?

The first space flight was made by Yuri Gagarin (USSR) in 1962. His flight lasted less than two hours.

Gagarin's spaceship went round the earth once.

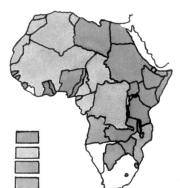

In 1969, people landed on the Moon for the first time.

9. Which country did the first people on the Moon come from?

What were the colonies?

In the first half of the 20th century, most of Africa and India were governed by European countries. The Europeans often took the best land and products for themselves. The countries they ruled were called colonies.

People in the colonies wanted to govern themselves. Some colonies had to fight their rulers before they won their independence.

Africa was divided up as follows:

Britain
France
Portugal
Belgium
Spain

Algeria fought its rulers for eight years before it won independence, in 1962.

10. Which country ruled Algeria before it won independence?

Djibouti was the last African country to gain independence, in 1977.

Megaquiz

Try these quizzes to see how much you can remember from the rest of the book. Write your answers down and then check on page 32 to see how many you got right.

Famous people

Match the descriptions of these ten famous people with their names, listed in the blue box below.

1. A scientist who developed the theory of evolution.
2. An Ancient Egyptian king who died aged 18.
3. A leader of the Moslem army during the Crusades.
4. The title given to the Aztec king.
5. The inventor of the first petrol-driven car.
6. The first person to fly a powered plane.
7. The leader of Germany in the 1930s and 1940s.
8. The scientist who was imprisoned for writing that the Earth travels round the Sun.
9. The last *tsar* of Russia.
10. The hero of Homer's epic poem, the *Odyssey.*

a) Adolf Hitler	c) Galileo	e) Nicholas II	g) Great Speaker	i) Karl Benz
b) Orville Wright	d) Odysseus	f) Tutankhamun	h) Saladin	j) Charles Darwin

Clothes and fashions

Who wore these costumes and hairstyles?

True or false?

1. The Ancient Romans used soap to get clean.
2. Viking warriors were buried or burned in ships.
3. Cowboys rode bicycles around cattle farms.
4. The first computer was smaller than this book.
5. The women's parts in Greek plays were played by men.
6. Dr Edward Jenner found a way to stop people from catching smallpox.
7. The car that the Ford Motor Company first sold in 1908 was called the Model X.
8. During a siege, castle dwellers were allowed out to fetch food and water.
9. Tenochtitlan, the Aztec capital, was built in the middle of a lake.
10. At the Greek sports festival in Olympia, winners received gold medals.

Which came first?

Can you put each set of three people, animals or things in order of appearance or invention?

1. Tyrannosaurus rex; Stegosaurus; jellyfish.
2. Viking; *conquistador*; Bolshevik.
3. Computer; steam engine; horse and cart.
4. Cannon; sword; six-shooter.
5. Tsar Nicholas II; Richard I; Tutankhamun.
6. Inoculation; television; water well.
7. Model T Ford; Viking longship; chariot.
8. Pyramid; Palace of Alhambra; nuclear power station.
9. Amelia Bloomer; Homer; Lenin.
10. USSR; Roman Empire; Inca Empire.

Close-ups

These are all close-ups of parts of pictures in the book. Can you recognize what they show?

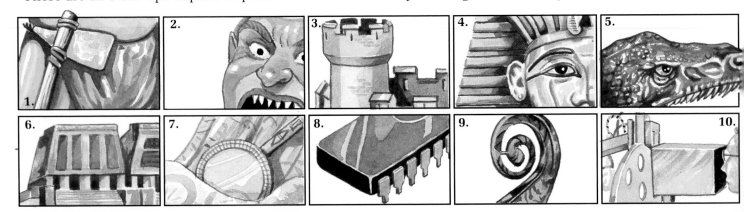

Where in the world?

Can you match the places marked on the map with the descriptions below?

1. Christopher Columbus was trying to sail to this country when he landed in America.
2. The Cultural Revolution took place in this country in the 1960s.
3. There was a nuclear accident here in 1986.
4. *Conquistadores* came from this country.
5. There are hieroglyphics in the tombs here.
6. The Aztecs used to live here.
7. A famous sports festival was held in this city.
8. The Circus Maximus was in this city.
9. The scientist Galileo lived in this country.
10. This country had the first passenger train service.

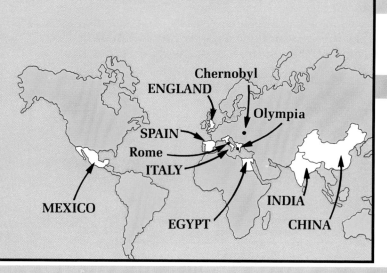

The time line

Can you match these events with the dates on the time line below?

1. Modern man first appears.
2. Homer the poet makes up the *Iliad*.
3. Spanish *conquistadores* attack the Aztecs.
4. Dinosaurs dominate the Earth.
5. Egyptians start building pyramids.
6. Rome is the most powerful city in Europe.
7. Vikings begin exploring the world.
8. The People's Crusade begins.
9. Cannons are invented.
10. The first people land on the Moon.

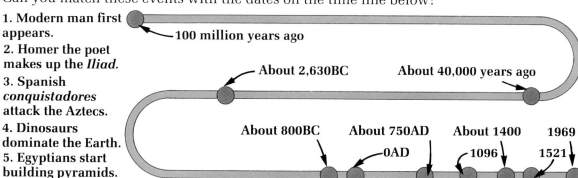

100 million years ago
About 2,630BC
About 40,000 years ago
About 800BC
About 750AD
About 1400
1969
0AD
1096
1521

What do you know?

1. Most Ancient Egyptians were not buried in pyramids. Where were they buried?
2. What lived on Earth until 65 million years ago?
3. Can you name a group of people who were not allowed to vote in Ancient Athens?
4. What was the name given to Viking story tellers?
5. Which company made the best-selling car ever?
6. *Tsar* is a Russian word. What does it mean?
7. What weapon gave European invaders a big advantage over the Aztecs and Incas?
8. Were the first TV pictures in colour or black and white?
9. Where might you find a loop, a crenel and a merlon?
10. When hunting, what did American Indians often wear to disguise themselves?

Silhouettes

All these silhouettes are of things that appear in the book. How many can you recognize?

   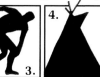   

What else do you know?

1. Which was the biggest dinosaur?
2. What country did the first man in space come from?
3. Besides comedies, what sort of plays could you watch at a Greek theatre?
4. What was in the Montgolfier brothers' balloon to make it rise?
5. On the tracks which crossed the Inca Empire, how long did it usually take travellers to walk from one rest house to another?
6. What did the Ancient Romans watch at the Colosseum?
7. What new type of fuel was used in power stations in the 1950s?
8. Did the Ancient Romans know how to make hot water?
9. Who led the Christian army against Saladin during the Crusades?
10. What was the name given to the huge cattle farms where cowboys worked?

Quiz answers

The answers to the 12 quizzes from *The dinosaur age* to *The twentieth century* are on the next four pages. Give yourself one point for every right answer. The chart below helps you to find out how well you have done.

0-3	Read through the answers, then try the quiz again. See how many answers you can remember second time around.
4-6	Quite good. Think carefully about the questions and you might get more answers right.
7-9	Good score. If you get this score on most of the quizzes, you can be very pleased with yourself.
10	Excellent. If you do this well in more than half the quizzes, you are a history genius!

Your score overall

You can find out your average score over all 12 quizzes like this:
1. Add up your scores on all 12 quizzes.
2. Divide this total by 12. This is your average score. How well did you do?

General knowledge

All the answers to general knowledge questions are marked ★. These questions are probably the hardest in the quizzes. Add up how many of them you got right across all 12 quizzes. There are 40 of them in total. If you got over 25 right, your general knowledge is good.

The dinosaur age

1. "Dinosaur" means (a) terrible lizard. The name is made up of the Greek words *deinos* (terrible) and *sauros* (lizard).
2. Stegosaurus used its tail as a weapon. (If you guessed that it was used for fighting, score a point.)
3. The name Tyrannosaurus rex means Tyrant Lizard King.
★ 4. Bones preserved in rock are called (b) fossils. The picture shows the fossilized skull of a Triceratops. The silhouette of a man shows you how big the skull was.
5. False. Brachiosaurus was too big to climb trees.
6. True. No dinosaur skins have been preserved. They were probably greenish or brownish to blend in with their backgrounds but no one knows the exact colour.
★ 7. Eight of the animals still exist, although they might look a bit different now from their prehistoric form. They are: crocodile, frog, tortoise, snake, ape, human, jellyfish and shrew. Only score a point if you spotted them all. If you spotted the shrew but did not get its name right, score a point anyway since it is difficult to identify.
★ 8. A meat eater is (a) a carnivore. A herbivore eats plants. An animal that eats meat and plants is called an omnivore.
9. No. The biggest dinosaur found so far is Brachiosaurus. These pictures show how big it was compared to T. rex.

10. (c) About 800 different kinds of dinosaur have been found so far.

Ancient Egypt

★ 1. There is still a country called Egypt. It has been called Egypt for nearly 5,000 years.

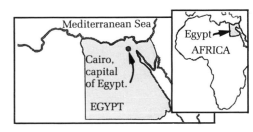

2. Embalmed bodies are known as (b) mummies. The word comes from the Arabic word *mum* which means bitumen (a sort of tar). A mummy's skin has a tarry look.
3. True. You can see mummies in some history museums.
4. (c) Elizabeth I was not a queen of Egypt. She was Queen of England from 1558 to 1603.
5. The pointed capstone went at the top of the pyramid.
6. The pyramids were covered with white limestone (see page 4). Most of this has now worn away or fallen off.
★ 7. Egyptian kings were called pharaohs. The name comes from the Ancient Egyptian expression *pr-o*, meaning "great house", or "palace".

Egyptian symbols for "pharaoh".

8. Egyptian children did not usually wear any clothes at all during the hot summer (see picture on page 5).
★ 9. The symbols on the wall were called (c) hieroglyphics. The name comes from the ancient Greek words *hieros* (sacred) and *glyphein* (to carve).
10. The symbol on the left means to walk. On the right are some other hieroglyphics and their meanings.

Water

Mouth

Ancient Greece

★ 1. Athens is the present capital of Greece (see map below).
2. On page 6, the mask on the left shows happiness and the other mask shows anger. (Score a point if you guessed other feelings similar to happiness and anger.)

Mask of a tragic heroine.

3. True. Olives were valuable to Greek farmers. They crushed them to make olive oil which they sold to foreign traders.
4. Homer's poems were called (a) epics. They were learned by heart and recited at parties. Epics were very long and might take hours to recite. For centuries they were not written down but were passed on by word of mouth.
★ 5. The model horse was made from wood.
6. Odysseus took (c) ten years to get home. Before he set out for Troy, he dreamed that he would not return for 20 years.

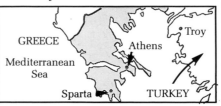

His dream came true: the siege of Troy lasted for ten years and then he took another ten years to get home. The map shows where Troy probably was.

7. From left to right the gods are: a) Poseidon; d) Athene; b) Aphrodite; c) Zeus.
8. True. This seems to be one luxury that the Spartans allowed themselves.
9. From left to right the sports are: discus throwing, wrestling, relay racing, javelin throwing.
★ 10. The Olympic Games are named after the sports festival at Olympia. This was held at Olympia until 395AD. The first modern Olympic Games were held in 1896 in Athens.

Ancient Rome

★ 1. Julius Caesar. He was an army general who became ruler of Rome in 49BC. He was murdered in 44BC by rivals who thought he had too much power.

The Roman Empire is shaded in grey.

★ 2. Rome is now the capital of Italy (see map).

3. The month of March is named after the Roman god Mars. All the names of the months come from Roman names or numbers. For example, January is named after Janus, the god of doors, who had two faces.

4. If spectators wanted a fighter to die, they gave a thumbs-down sign. If they wanted a fighter to be allowed to live, they gave a thumbs-up sign.

Live · Die

5. The fighters were called (a) gladiators. The word is based on the Roman word *gladius*, meaning sword.

6. True. The largest soccer stadium in the world, the Maracana Stadium in Brazil, holds 205,000 people.

Maracana Stadium · Circus Maximus

7. At the baths, there are slaves giving a massage, plucking hair and tending the furnace. (Only score a point if you noticed all three.)

8. The building is the toilet block. Roman public toilets did not have cubicles.

★ 9. The Ancient Romans spoke (a) Latin. Latin is not spoken as a language nowadays but many European languages contain words which developed from Latin.

10. False. Roman men wore tunics or togas. Togas were for formal wear. They were made out of a piece of cloth 5m (15ft) in diameter (see picture on the right). This amount of material made them heavy. Tunics were much lighter and easier to wear.

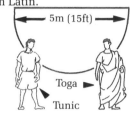
5m (15ft) · Toga · Tunic

The Vikings

★ 1. The Vikings came from the lands which are now the countries of Denmark, Norway and Sweden. This whole area is now called Scandinavia. Score a point if you got any of these.

Sweden · Norway · Denmark

2. Vikings used swords most often. They even gave their swords names, such as Fierce One and Leg Biter.

3. One Viking has been killed.

★ 4. The hole in the roof let smoke from a fire inside the house escape. The fire was lit in the middle of the house to provide warmth and for cooking.

Viking sword · Fire

5. Vikings could make their ships move in two ways.

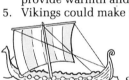
When it was windy they used a sail.

Score a point if you got either of these right.

When it was calm they rowed the ship.

6. Viking stories were called (a) sagas. A saga recited by a bard might last as long as a feature film does nowadays.

7. The name Viking comes from (b) the Viking word for adventurer. Every summer the Vikings set out on long sea journeys to look for trade or to raid coastal towns and villages in search of treasure.

★ 8. North America was further away from the Vikings' home than Ireland.

9. Viking heaven was called (a) Valhalla. It meant "the palace of the killed".

10. Thursday is named after Thor, the Viking god of thunder. The rest of the weekdays are named after the following:

Sunday: the Sun.
Monday: the Moon.
Tuesday: Tyr, the Viking god of law.
Wednesday: Odin, the Viking god of war.
Friday: Frigg, the Viking goddess of love.
Saturday: Saturn, the Roman god of farming.

The Crusades

1. The wall around Jerusalem was there for defence. (Score a point if you got the general idea.)

★ 2. Jesus Christ was born in Bethlehem.

3. True. Most of the People's Crusaders died from disease or lack of food. Some died in fights on the way to Palestine.

4. True. Moslems rode small Arab horses which could dart around the battlefield. The Crusaders' horses were heavier and slower. They had to carry a knight in full armour.

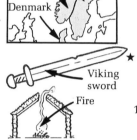

5. Saladin's sword was called (a) a scimitar. The Crusaders' swords, called broadswords, were heavier.

Scimitar
Broadsword

★ 6. Richard I was called "the Lionheart" because of his courage. Lions are supposed to be brave animals.

7. The Crusaders did not take (b) potatoes back to Europe. These were first taken to Europe from America by European sailors about 300 years after the Crusades.

8. The numbers as they appear from left to right are 1, 4, 7 and 9. Here is the whole set of numbers used by Moslem mathematicians, from 0 to 9.

0 1 2 3 4 5 6 7 8 9

9. True. The Moslems ruled lands on the continents of Africa, Asia and Europe.

★ 10. The game is chess. It was first played in northern India around the year 500AD. During the 11th and 12th centuries, India was invaded by Moslems. The Moslems learned to play chess and the game became popular all over the Moslem Empire.

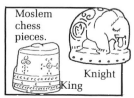
Moslem chess pieces. · King · Knight

A medieval castle

1. The defenders got drinking water from a well inside the castle. Its position in the picture on page 14 is shown here.

Well

2. The fortified gatehouse is called (c) a barbican.
3. The holes are called (a) murder holes. If attackers broke into the castle and went under the murder holes, the defenders fired at them through the holes or poured boiling liquid down on to them.
4. False. Some castle sieges lasted up to a year. Sometimes whole cities were besieged: a city could hold out longer than a castle. The siege of Acre in Palestine in 1189 was one of the longest. It lasted for two years.
5. The explosive that fired a cannon was (b) gunpowder. Dynamite was not invented until 1865, about 500 years after the cannon.

6. True. The Chinese invented gunpowder about 1,200 years ago.
★ 7. The order of invention is: spear (c), mangonel (a), tank (b). Spears have been used for thousands of years. An early type of mangonel was built by the Ancient Greeks. Tanks were first used in 1916, during World War I.
★ 8. This sort of bridge is called a drawbridge. It could be drawn up so that there was no bridge across the moat.

Drawbridge down   Drawbridge up

★ 9. The siege weapon is called a battering ram. Once across the moat (see below), the attackers used it to break down the castle gates.
★ 10. The deep channel of water is called a moat. Early castles were often built on a man-made mound of earth. The earth was dug from a circular trench which was usually filled with water to make a moat. The word "moat" comes from the old French word *mote*, meaning "mound".

The Aztecs and the Incas

1. True. Incas bred guinea pigs to eat during religious festivals.

2. The capital of Mexico is (b) Mexico City. It is the biggest city in the world. Part of it is built on the site of the old city of Tenochtitlan.

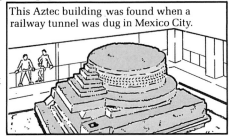

This Aztec building was found when a railway tunnel was dug in Mexico City.

3. The Aztecs thought that (a) a warrior was more important than a farmer or weaver. You can tell this by looking at his clothes which are grander than the clothes of the farmer and weaver.
4. True. They also made a red dye, called cochineal, out of crushed beetles and a green dye out of boiled tree bark.
5. The rug is worth more than the bird. That is why the bird-seller is offering cocoa beans as part of the deal.
6. The god in the picture is the Aztec god of war. He is carrying weapons such as a sword and an axe.

7. Swapping goods instead of selling them is called (a) bartering. The picture shows some examples of what cocoa beans were worth.

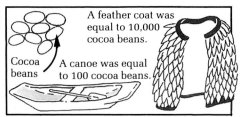

A feather coat was equal to 10,000 cocoa beans.

Cocoa beans   A canoe was equal to 100 cocoa beans.

★ 8. The bird is (c) a turkey. Until the Spaniards invaded South America, turkeys were only found in America . The Spanish *conquistadores* took turkeys back to Europe with them.
★ 9. It is a llama. Llamas came from the part of the Inca kingdom now called Peru.

Peru
SOUTH AMERICA

An Inca's llama brooch.

★ 10. Today, most South Americans speak (b) Spanish. Most of the rest speak Portuguese. Only a few speak the South American languages that their ancestors spoke before the Europeans invaded.

Inventions and discoveries

1. The trousers were called bloomers, after Amelia Bloomer.
★ 2. The man is wearing a top hat.
3. Saturn. (It is labelled in the picture above on page 18.)
★ 4. Galileo was right. Galileo developed the telescope and was able to watch the planets. He was the first to see the planet Saturn, in 1610. As more powerful telescopes were invented, people were able to see planets even further away. Uranus was seen in 1781, Neptune in 1846 and Pluto in 1930.

Galileo's telescope

★ 5. Steam engines pulled trains, powered ships and early types of car. They were also used to power machinery in mines. Score a point if you got any of these.

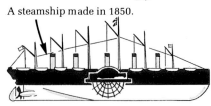

A steamship made in 1850.

6. The first regular TV broadcasts were made in (b) 1936. The first colour broadcast was in 1953.
7. True. Dairymaids often caught cowpox from the cows they milked. Jenner noticed that once they had caught cowpox they hardly ever got smallpox.
   Inoculation involves being injected with or swallowing a substance called a vaccine. This gives you a mild form of the illness. This stimulates your body's own defence system which protects you from later attacks of that disease.
8. (c) a cold cannot be prevented by inoculation. Here are some more diseases, though, which can be prevented by inoculation: chicken pox, polio, whooping cough, typhoid and cholera.
9. The birds are all types of (a) finch.
★ 10. The correct order of invention is: b) steam power; c) electricity; a) nuclear power. The first steam engine was made in about 1700. The first electric power was produced by a battery made in 1800. Nuclear power was first demonstrated in 1942.

The first electric battery looked like this.

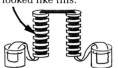

The Wild West

★ 1. The Indian tent on page 20 is a teepee. Score a point if you said teepee or wigwam, though, since many Indians lived in wigwams.

There is a wigwam shown above: they were often covered with leaves and branches.

2. For good luck in battle, Indians danced (b) a wardance.

3. The cattle are (c) longhorn cattle.

4. True. Horses were taken to America by Spanish conquerors about 500 years ago. American Indians tamed and rode the horses that escaped from the Spaniards.

★ 5. It is a lasso or lariat. This is a rope with a loop tied with a sliding knot. If something inside the loop tugs the rope, the knot tightens round it.

Sliding knot

6. The Indians called (a) guns "smoke sticks".

★ 7. Canada and the USA make up North America. Only score a point if you got them both right. The other countries are in South America.

Canada. Alaska is part of the USA. NORTH AMERICA. USA

8. Most cowboys wore (a) stetsons.

9. The pistol was called a six-shooter because it fired six shots before it had to be reloaded.
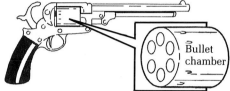
Bullet chamber

★ 10. Cowboys branded cattle so that they could tell who the cattle belonged to. If cattle were stolen, brands helped people to identify them and return them to their owner. Cattle thieves were called rustlers.

Trains, cars and planes

1. There are seven different forms of transport on pages 22-23: horse and carriage, train, horseback, car, balloon, plane and airship. Only score a point if you spotted all seven.

2. True. A galloping horse can travel at 45kmph (28mph). The first trains went at about 20kmph (12mph).

3. The Russian Empire is now known as (a) the USSR. You can find out why the name changed on page 24.

★ 4. A modern car company that uses Karl Benz's name is Mercedes-Benz. A car made by Mercedes-Benz has the badge shown on the right on the bonnet.

★ 5. The handle, called a crank, was used to start the engine. It had to be turned rapidly. The first car that had a starter motor was made by Cadillac in 1912.

1912 Cadillac

6. For several years the Ford Model T was only available in (b) black. For speed, Ford used quick-drying paint, which was only made in black. In 1923, paint manufacturers began to make quick-drying paints in other colours.

★ 7. The car is a Beetle, or Bug (score a point for either name). Volkswagen have built over 20 million of these since they were first made in 1936.

8. Air-filled tyres are called (a) pneumatic tyres. The word comes from the Greek word *pneuma*, meaning "breath".

★ 9. Modern planes are made out of steel. Thin steel sheets are attached to a steel frame. The fastest passenger jet, Concorde, can fly at around 2,400kmph (1,500mph).
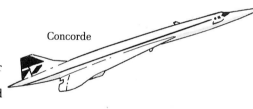
Concorde

10. False. Airships crashed quite often.

The twentieth century

1. The Bolshevik flag was red. You can see one in the first picture on page 24. The communist government later put a hammer and sickle on the flag. These represented the tools used by industrial workers and rural peasants and symbolized links between them.

2. True. Nicholas II was the last tsar. His palace, the Kremlin, is now the home of the USSR's government.

The Kremlin

★ 3. The Nazi leader was Adolf Hitler. He became *Führer* (leader) of Germany in 1933. He killed himself in 1945 when the Nazis lost World War II.

4. World War II lasted for six years, from 1939-1945. More than 50 million people died during it. That is about as many people as live in Australia, Canada and Holland.

5. There have been (a) two World Wars. World War I lasted from 1914-1918.

6. A war between people of the same country is called (b) a civil war.

★ 7. The USSR was the first country to have a communist government. Score a point if you guessed USSR, Russia or the Russian Empire.

8. It is called (c) a chip.

★ 9. The first people to walk on the Moon came from the USA. Between 1969-1972, six US missions explored the Moon. The last two missions took vehicles, called lunar rovers, with them. The lunar rovers are still on the Moon.
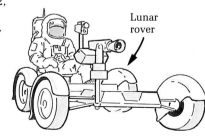
Lunar rover

10. Algeria was ruled by France before it won independence in 1962.

Megaquiz answers

There are 100 possible points in the whole Megaquiz. If you score over 50 you have done well. Over 75 is excellent. You can find out more about each answer on the page listed after it.

Famous people

1. (j) Charles Darwin (page 19).
2. (f) Tutankhamun (page 5).
3. (h) Saladin (page 13).
4. (g) Great Speaker (page 16).
5. (i) Karl Benz (page 22).
6. (b) Orville Wright (page 23).
7. (a) Adolf Hitler (page 24).
8. (c) Galileo (page 18).
9. (e) Nicholas II (page 24).
10. (d) Odysseus (pages 6 and 7).

Clothes and fashions

1. Anubis or Egyptian priest (page 4).
2. Crusader (pages 12 and 13).
3. Amelia Bloomer (page 18).
4. Aztec (page 17).
5. Cowboy (pages 20 and 21).
6. Roman (pages 8 and 9).
7. American Indian (page 20).
8. Egyptian (page 4).
9. Greek or Spartan soldier (page 7).
10. Viking (pages 10 and 11).

True or false?

1. False (page 8).
2. True (page 11).
3. False (page 20).
4. False (page 25).
5. True (page 6).
6. True (page 19).
7. False (page 23).
8. False (page 15).
9. True (page 16).
10. False (page 7).

Which came first?

1. Jellyfish; Stegosaurus; T. rex.
2. Viking; *conquistador*; Bolshevik.
3. Horse and cart; steam engine; computer.
4. Sword; cannon; six-shooter.
5. Tutankhamun; Richard I; Nicholas II.
6. Water well; inoculation; television.
7. Chariot; Viking longship; Model T Ford.
8. Pyramid; Palace of Alhambra; nuclear power station.
9. Homer; Amelia Bloomer; Lenin.
10. Roman Empire; Inca Empire; USSR.

Close-ups

1. Tomahawk (page 20).
2. Greek actor's mask (page 6).
3. Castle (page 14).
4. Tutankhamun's mask (page 5).
5. Tyrannosaurus rex (page 3).
6. Aztec Great Temple (page 17).
7. Mirror (page 13).
8. Computer chip (page 25).
9. Viking longship (page 11).
10. Early television (page 18).

Where in the world?

1. India (page 21).
2. China (page 25).
3. Chernobyl (page 19).
4. Spain (page 17).
5. Egypt (page 5).
6. Mexico (page 16).
7. Olympia (page 7).
8. Rome (page 9).
9. Italy (page 18).
10. England (page 22).

The time line

1. About 40,000 years ago (page 3).
2. About 800BC (page 6).
3. 1521 (page 17).
4. 100 million years ago (page 2).
5. About 2,630BC (pages 4 and 5).
6. 0AD (page 8).
7. About 750AD (pages 10 and 11).
8. 1096 (page 12).
9. About 1400 (page 15).
10. 1969 (page 25).

What do you know?

1. In the sand (page 5).
2. Dinosaurs (page 2).
3. Women or slaves. Score a point for either (page 6).
4. Bards (page 11).
5. Volkswagen (page 23).
6. Emperor (page 24).
7. The gun (page 17).
8. Black and white (page 18).
9. A castle (page 14).
10. Animal skins (page 20).

Silhouettes

1. Dinosaur or Parasaurolophus (page 3).
2. Power station (page 19).
3. Greek athlete (page 7).
4. Teepee or wigwam (page 20).
5. Benz's car or early car (page 22).
6. Finch or bird (page 19).
7. Mangonel (page 15).
8. Roman chariot (page 9).
9. Pyramids (pages 4 and 5).
10. Invicta or steam engine (page 22).

What else do you know?

1. Brachiosaurus (page 2).
2. USSR (page 25).
3. Tragedies (page 6).
4. Hot air (page 23).
5. One day (page 16).
6. Fights, or the Games (pages 8 and 9).
7. Nuclear fuel (page 19).
8. Yes (page 8).
9. Richard I or "the Lionheart" (page 13).
10. Ranches (pages 20).

Index

First published in 1991 by Usborne Publishing Ltd, Usborne House, 83-85 Saffron Hill, London EC1N 8RT, England. Copyright © Usborne Publishing Ltd 1991

The name Usborne and the device ♉ are Trade Marks of Usborne Publishing Ltd.